BREAST CANCER

BREAST CANCER

Elaine Landau

A Venture Book
FRANKLIN WATTS
A Division of Grolier Publishing
New York London Hong Kong Sydney
Danbury, Connecticut

For Janet Bode

Photographs copyright ©: Ben Klaffke: pp. 10, 20, 22, 24, 27, 34, 55, 59, 63, 68, 72, 75, 78, 80, 86, 95; National Cancer Institute: pp. 15, 61, 66; NYU Medical Center: p. 31; American Cancer Society: p. 36; American College of Radiology/Hilary Schwab: p. 44; Jim West: p. 90.

Library of Congress Cataloging-in-Publication Data

Landau, Elaine.
Breast cancer / by Elaine Landau.
p.   cm. — (A Venture book)
Includes bibliographical references and index.
ISBN 0-531-11242-X
1. Breast—Cancer. (1. Breast—Cancer. 2. Cancer. 3. Diseases.)
I. Title.
RC280.B8L275 1995
616.99'449—dc20   95-3831 CIP AC

CONTENTS

BREAST CANCER

INTRODUCTION: SHANA SPEAKS, AGE 17

Two weeks before my sixteenth birthday my mother had a mammogram that the doctor thought looked suspicious. He said she'd have to go to the hospital for a biopsy to see if the lump were malignant. No one in my family wanted to say the word out loud, but we weren't strangers to breast cancer. Three years ago my grandmother died of it, and the disease killed my aunt the following year. Ever since then, my mother had gone for mammograms. But we just thought of it as a precaution. My mother was still young and it was hard for me to think that she might have a life-threatening disease.

I heard about breast cancer for the first time when I was nine and had gone to the beach with an older cousin. A woman there wore a bathing suit with short sleeves, and I'd never seen swimwear like

Young girls like the one seen here shopping for lingerie rarely develop breast cancer, but their lives may be dramatically affected by the disease if their mothers or other close family members are stricken with it.

that before. When I asked my cousin about it, she told me that those swimsuits were for women who'd had a breast removed. As I got older and heard the public service announcements for mammograms, I wondered what it would be like to lose one or both of my breasts.

Some men don't think of females as feminine, desirable, or even as *women* without breasts. I hated being flat-chested when I was twelve and couldn't wait to get my first bra and be able to fill it. When that time finally came, my mother went with me to the lingerie shop. The saleswoman brought out an assortment of undergarments—all of them had ribbons, satin, or lace. Seeing that I was impressed, she asked, "Are these pretty enough? Young, pretty girls should have pretty bras." She'd said that I was pretty and now I was buying a pretty bra. Somehow having breasts had magically transformed me from a girl to a woman. It felt like I had just crossed over a major threshold. I was suddenly grown up and maybe even alluring.

As we developed breasts, the boys at school began to notice the change. They'd sneak up on us, snap our bra straps and run. If you wore a light-colored or mesh blouse during the summer, they' stare at your top, trying to catch a glimpse of what was beneath. Two girls in our class were especially well-endowed and the boys teased yet admired them. They got more offers for dates than any of us. My girlfriends and I said that breasts that large weren't fashionable, but we'd have traded ours for theirs in a heartbeat. It hadn't taken us long to realize that

11

breasts were considered an important part of what made women sexy, and in demand.

I think that's why breast cancer is so scary. It's worse than just a deadly disease—it forces women to battle for their lives, then leaves many survivors permanently disfigured in the eyes of some. I can't imagine being afraid you'll die and at the same time worrying that if you live you won't appeal to your boyfriend or husband anymore. I think my mother might have felt that way when she went in for her biopsy.

My mother had always been a healthy, vital woman with a figure my father and others admired. She took tremendous pride in her appearance. I used to watch her do her face and hair. She worked at it meticulously, as if she were adding the final touches to a painting. Then she'd slip into an outfit that showed off the body she'd spent hours working on at the gym.

How could a woman like that have breast cancer? It may sound childish, but at first I kept telling myself that this can't be happening because mothers don't get sick. When I thought about the pain she might go through, I wanted to do something heroic, but I couldn't think of anything. I tried to picture what it would be like to have a very sick mom instead of the beautiful, capable woman who'd always cared for us. But the most frightening thought of all was that I might end up not having a mother at all.

1

DIAGNOSING BREAST CANCER

Breast cancer is part of my past and possibly part of my future, but it's certainly not who I am. And while I don't expect to live forever, one can always hope.[1]

—Linda Ellerbee, TV producer

Breast cancer is a frightening disease. It can be fatal, and while two thirds of the cases occur among mature women, it also strikes younger females and about nine thousand males each year. The fear generated by breast cancer is intensified by the somewhat shocking reality that breast cancer has actually increased over the last fifty years. In 1940, a woman had a one-in-twenty chance of developing the disease, while today one out of every eight women will get breast cancer. According to the National Cancer Institute, every three minutes somewhere a woman is diagnosed with it. Yet despite the recent breast's lobules—a subdivision of the breast's lobes that are arranged like the petal of a daisy.

Although more than 180,000 American woman are diagnosed with breast cancer annually, scientists still aren't certain why one woman develops the disease and not another. So far researchers know that breast cancer is not caused by bumping or bruising the breast and that an individual cannot "catch" breast cancer from someone who already has the disease. A number of risk factors have been isolated that are thought to increase an individual's chances of having breast cancer. They are as follows:

RISK FACTORS

AGE

A woman's risk of getting breast cancer increases with age. Approximately 75 percent of all breast cancer occurs among women over fifty years old, while breast cancer in females under twenty is relatively rare. The National Cancer Institute chart illustrates the dramatic correlation between advanced age and breast cancer.

Some researchers argue that although older women have an increased risk for breast cancer, a close examination of how these figures were derived reveals that the prospects may not be as grim as they seem. In 1991, the American Cancer Society noted that women who live to be eighty-five have a one-in-nine possibility of developing

CHANCES OF DEVELOPING BREAST CANCER

By age 25:	one in 21,441
By age 30:	one in 2,426
By age 35:	one in 622
By age 40:	one in 222
By age 45:	one in 96
By age 50:	one in 52
By age 55:	one in 34
By age 60:	one in 24
By age 65:	one in 18
By age 70:	one in 14
By age 75:	one in 12
By age 80:	one in 10
By age 85:	one in 9
Ever:	one in 8
Age 20 to 30:	one in 2,415
30 to 40:	one in 240
40 to 50:	one in 66
50 to 60:	one in 43
60 to 70:	one in 29
70 to 80:	one in 25

Source: NCI Surveillance Program

breast cancer. On the other hand, the following year the National Cancer Institute estimated that a female living ninety-five or more years has a one-in-eight chance of getting the disease.[2] In actuality, however, the life expectancy of a woman in the United States is neither eighty-five nor over ninety-five, but seventy-nine years of age. Therefore, her genuine risk for breast cancer may be somewhat lower.

MEDICAL HISTORY

Certain facts in a women's medical history may put her at higher risk for breast cancer. Women who've had breast cancer in the past have a greater chance of getting the disease again. This doesn't mean that the initial cancer will necessarily recur but rather that the woman has a greater likelihood of developing another distinct cancer. The National Cancer Institute cites that about 15 percent of the women who've had breast cancer will have a second breast cancer at a later date.

FAMILY HISTORY

The chances of developing breast cancer increase if a woman's mother, sister, or daughter either has the disease or has previously had breast cancer. The risk is even greater if the relative had cancer in both breasts or if it developed prior to menopause.

As Dr. Kenneth Offit, Director of Clinical Genetics at Memorial Sloan-Kettering Cancer Center noted:

> *About 20 percent of women with newly diagnosed breast cancer have a first degree or second degree relative [a grandmother is considered a second degree relative] with breast cancer . . . . If you have a first degree relative—unless the rela-*

tive is elderly—your risk is probably twice that of someone who doesn't have a first-degree relative with breast cancer. Perhaps only five percent of breast cancer is strictly inherited, but this accounts for about 40 percent of all breast cancers that appear before age 30.[3]

AGE AT FIRST MENSTRUATION

Females who begin menstruating at an early age (before twelve) are more likely to develop breast cancer than are other women.

AGE AT MENOPAUSE

Women who undergo a late menopause (over fifty-five years of age) are at a greater risk for breast cancer.

PREGNANCY

Pregnancy has been shown to affect a women's breast-cancer risk. Women who've had a child before thirty are less likely to develop breast cancer than those who either had their first child later on or were never pregnant. This isn't so, however, for women under thirty whose pregnancies were terminated through abortion. One study, conducted at the Fred Hutchinson Cancer Research Center in Seattle, Washington, involving 1,800 women over a seven-year period, indicated that having an abortion can increase a female's risk of developing breast cancer. Further research must be done, however, before scientists can be certain of a connection between abortion and breast cancer.

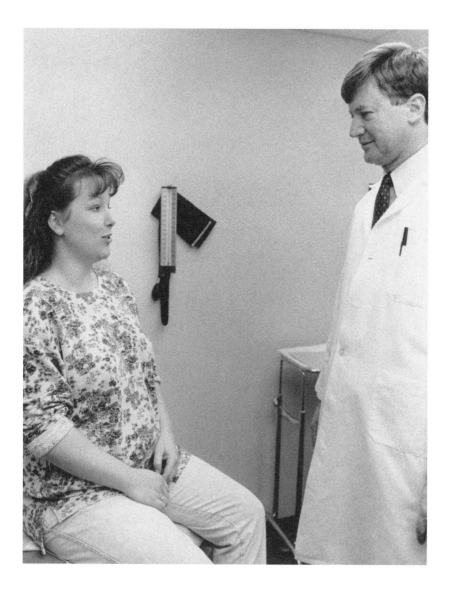

A young pregnant woman visits her physician for prenatal care. Women who either don't have children or have their first child after age thirty are thought to be at higher risk for breast cancer.

DIET

Although the results are not conclusive, current research suggests that women whose diets are high in fat are more likely to develop breast cancer. This conclusion was partially based on studies of Japanese families who left Japan (where incidence of breast cancer is exceedingly low) to come to America. Researchers tracking them found that the breast cancer rate among females increased with subsequent generations until it equaled that of the general U.S. population.

In Japan, the typical diet contains less than 20 percent fat, while in the United States the rate is often 35 percent. The longer the Japanese families remained in the United States, the more mainstream their eating habits became, which might help account for the subsequent increase in breast cancer. The researchers further found that countries with typically high fat consumption, such as the United States and numerous western European nations, tend to have considerably more breast cancer than do Third World nations where diets usually have a lower fat content. However, other studies undercut this reasoning. The Nurses Health Study, an eight-year project conducted by Harvard University and involving nearly 40,600 women, found no difference in the incidence of breast cancer among women with either high- or low-fat diets.

New research suggests that still other dietary aspects may influence breast-cancer levels. A number of studies indicate that women who drink

A traditional Asian diet, including vegetables rich in vitamin A and beta-carotene, might lower a woman's risk of developing breast cancer as well as other health problems.

alcohol may be slightly more likely to develop the disease. It's thought that the risk escalates in accordance with the amount consumed.

HORMONES

There's some research to suggest that estrogen, a hormone manufactured by a woman's ovaries and to a lesser extent by her fat tissue, influences her chances of having breast cancer. Evidence of the relationship between estrogen and breast cancer was discerned as early as 1892, when physicians noted that women with breast cancer who had their ovaries removed frequently experienced a remission of the disease. Women who have hysterectomies at a young age involving the removal of their ovaries also tend to have significantly less breast cancer.

During the initial phase of a woman's menstrual cycle, estrogen causes the cells lining one or both breasts' ducts to increase—possibly encouraging tumor development. This effect has been heightened in recent times because today women are exposed to estrogen's effects for significantly longer periods than in the past. In the United States the average age at which a girl begins menstruating is twelve, while two centuries ago it was seventeen. Women also reach menopause later today (at about fifty-two years old) than they did a century ago. Researcher Malcolm C. Pike of the University of Southern California School of Medicine estimates that modern women may ovulate 450 times during their lives, while their ancestors ovulated only about 150 times. If repeated cyclical exposure to

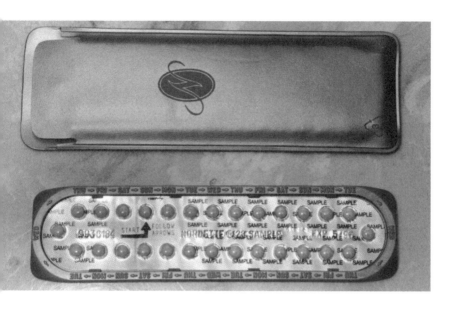

Some studies indicate that women who take oral contraceptives (birth control pills) have a lower incidence of cancer of the ovaries and endometrium (the uterus lining). But other research suggests that the pills may increase the risk for cervical cancer.

estrogen enhances the possibility of breast cancer, modern women are clearly more vulnerable to the disease.

Some scientists suspect that medications containing hormones such as birth control pills or estrogen replacement to alleviate menopausal symptoms may heighten a women's risk for breast cancer if taken for prolonged periods. As this has not been definitely proved, however, significant numbers of women are still participating in hormone related research.

LIFESTYLE STATUS

Breast cancer is more prevalent among women with high incomes and educational levels.

RACE AND ETHNIC ORIGIN

Jewish women and women whose roots can be traced to the Mediterranean area may be at higher risk for breast cancer. Some research indicates that although breast cancer is more common among white than African-American females, women of color are more likely to die as a result of the disease. While this discrepancy was previously believed to be a result of lower income levels and poor access in African-American communities to medical care, it's now thought that black women may actually be susceptible to a more deadly type of breast cancer.

In one study, in which all the participants belonged to health-maintenance organizations affording them the same level of care, black women's tumors tended to be more advanced at the time of diagnosis, suggesting a faster growth rate. A second study, conducted at the University of Texas Health Science Center, in San Antonio, examined more than six thousand breast cancer tumors sent to them from hospitals throughout the United States. The researchers found that the tumors received from black women tended to have more actively dividing cells. Still another research project revealed that a particularly devastating form of the disease appears to strike black females under forty-five years of age.

RADIATION

Research studies have confirmed the link between radiation and an increased risk of developing breast cancer. The women surveyed had been exposed to exceedingly high levels of radiation as the result of either atomic bombings or medical procedures entailing massive radiation doses.

SMOKING

A 1994 study indicated that female smokers face a greater risk of dying of breast cancer than do non-smokers. The research, involving 600,000 women over a six-year period, showed that the risk rose in direct proportion to the number of cigarettes used and the length of time the woman smoked.

The research, however, did not assert that smoking is a direct cause of breast cancer or that smokers are more likely to develop the disease. Rather, it suggests that female smokers may suffer from impaired immune responses or other health problems that compromise their survival chances if stricken with breast cancer.

ENVIRONMENTAL CONTAMINANTS

Recent evidence suggests that there may be a link between breast cancer and environmental toxins. A research team, led by University of Michigan physician and toxicologist Frank Falck, Jr., tested forty women who had breast lumps surgically removed. The team analyzed fatty tissues from the breasts of both the women with malignancies and those whose growths had been benign. The pa-

Although smoking doesn't cause breast cancer, it can weaken a woman's ability to fight the disease. Instead of smoking, these women might be better off going for a walk together.

tients with cancerous tumors had 50 to 60 percent higher concentrations of contaminants—such as DDT, a pesticide, and a class of industrial chemicals known as polychlorinated biphenyls (PCBs).

Other research revealed that some pollutants, dubbed "environmental estrogens," act similarly to the hormone estrogen encouraging breast cells to divide while possibly promoting tumor development. Test-tube studies further showed that some environmental estrogens caused cells to produce an estrogen by-product that may foster malignancies. So far a sprinkling of these estrogen "act-alikes" have triggered breast cancer in lab animals.

The possible role of environmental contaminants in breast cancer has caused a good deal of concern among women. While some of these questionable products have been banned for use in the United States, many have accumulated in the bodies and remain in the fat stores of women who were exposed to them significantly earlier. In response to the public outcry over the exceedingly high incidence of breast cancer on Long Island, New York, the New York State Department of Health investigated the possible association between residing near industries and high-traffic areas and the risk of breast cancer. The finding identified a correlation between postmenopausal women and the number and proximity of chemical facilities to their homes. In studying women who lived in the area for an extended period, the research further indicated that the association was more pronounced from 1965 to 1975, compared to 1975 to 1985, when state air-pollution control standards were strengthened.

The researchers involved with the Long Island study stressed that their sample population was small and that further studies are needed. But other scientists, accessing this data along with additional information, feel we cannot afford to wait for conclusive evidence to take action. They want the government to ban pesticides that imitate estrogen before these products are approved and marketed to the public. One cell biologist at Tufts University School of Medicine urged, "Let's be careful. . . . Do we need all the pesticides out there?"[4] Still other scientists remain skeptical of these proposals, underscoring the need for more research. They argue that such environmental contaminants are more likely to be promoters or inducers of the disease than direct carcinogens.

Unfortunately, in evaluating risk factors for breast cancer, our knowledge is still incomplete. As Dr. Susan Love, breast cancer specialist and founding director of the UCLA Breast Center noted, "You have to be careful when you talk about risk factors, because we don't know what all of them are. We've been able to isolate a few, but they're not very predictive. We can't say, 'You women here in this group are at high risk and you over there in that other group are home free.' Some 70 percent of the women who develop breast cancer have no risk factors at all."[5]

SYMPTOMS OF BREAST CANCER

Unfortunately, during the early stages of breast cancer, there may be no discernable symptoms. Often women think they are cancer-free because they haven't experienced any discomfort, but initially breast cancer is painless. That's why it's important for women to examine their own breasts for irregularities each month as well as have their breasts checked regularly by a doctor or nurse.

The health care professional will check the patient's breasts both while she is sitting and lying down. She may be asked to raise her hands above her head, press her hands against her skin, or let them rest at her sides. The person examining her will be looking for such skin changes on the breast as dimpling, scaling, or puckering. He or she will also check for any discharge from the nipple or change in breast size or shape. The health care professional will use the pads of his or her fingers to feel for lumps throughout the breast, underarm, and collarbone area. In most cases, a lump will be the size of a pea when detected during such an examination.

Women practicing breast self-examination (BSE) at home should remember that every woman's breasts are different. Breasts also change as a woman grows older, because of pregnancy, menopause, taking birth control pills or other hormones, or even as a result of her menstrual cycle. A women whose breasts feel lumpy, uneven, or swollen and tender during her menstrual cycle need not necessarily be concerned about breast cancer. By consistently examining her breasts each month, however, she'll learn what is normal for her and be alert to unusual changes.

The American Cancer Society suggests that women begin breast self-examination at twenty, even though the disease is unlikely to occur at such a young age. Breast surgeon Dr. Peter Pressman explained why this head start is desirable: "Women

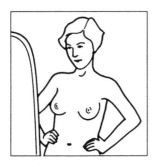

IN FRONT OF A MIRROR
With arms at your sides, inspect each breast carefully. Look for any changes in size, shape, and contour, or any puckering, dimpling, or change in skin texture. Gently squeeze each nipple and look for any discharge.

Repeat with your arms raised above your head.

LYING DOWN
Place a pillow under your right shoulder, and your right hand behind your head. Examine your right breast with your left hand. with fingers flat, gently press in a circular motion, starting at the outside top edge and spiraling toward the nipple. Include your underarm and the area below your breast.

Repeat for your left breast.

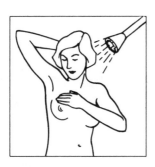

IN THE SHOWER
Raise your right arm and use your left hand to examine your right breast. With fingers flat, using a circular motion, touch every part of the breast, including the underarm, gently feeling for a lump or thickening.

Repeat for your left breast.

*Females should examine their own breasts
at the same time each month.*

should start a habit of regular breast self-examination in their late teens or early twenties, when it's not so threatening. If you start at fifty you have more reasons to be fearful, but it's still advisable."[6]

When performing breast self-examination, women should be alert to the following possible cancer warning signs:

- a lump or thickening of tissue in or around the breast or the underarm area.
- any change in breast size or shape.
- a difference in skin color or texture on any part of the breast.

Although such changes do not necessarily mean that a woman has breast cancer, it's important that she see her doctor to make certain.

DIAGNOSIS

In checking for breast cancer, a woman's doctor should both take a complete medical history and do a thorough physical exam. Besides ascertaining her overall well-being, the physician may rely on one or more of the breast exams described below to arrive at a diagnosis.

PALPATION

Through palpation (feeling the lump and surrounding tissue) the physician can learn a great deal about the growth. Round smooth lumps that move easily when held between two fingers are usually not malignant. On the other hand, hard jagged-shaped lumps that feel firmly attached within the breast are more likely to be cancerous.

MAMMOGRAPHY

A mammogram is composed of two separate X rays of the breast—a side view and a top view, together revealing a great deal about any growths or irregularities uncovered. In some cases, a mammogram can detect a breast lump while it's still too small to feel. Mammograms may also detect tiny calcium deposits known as microcalcification, which can be an early sign of breast cancer.

In taking these pictures, the breast is positioned between two plates pressed together to flatten the breast as much as possible. Flattening the breast spreads out the tissue, making abnormalities or suspicious areas easier to detect using a minimum of radiation. Because the pressure from the plates may cause some slight discomfort, mammograms should be scheduled just after the woman's menstrual cycle, when her breasts are less likely to be tender or sore.

While some women have expressed concern about exposure to radiation through mammograms, the risk involved is extremely low. Federal guidelines limit the amount of radiation used for both views of a breast to one rad (rad stands for "radiation absorbed dose"). But in actuality, most mammograms give off only a fraction of this amount.

After the mammogram is checked by the technologist taking it, a radiologist (a physician special-

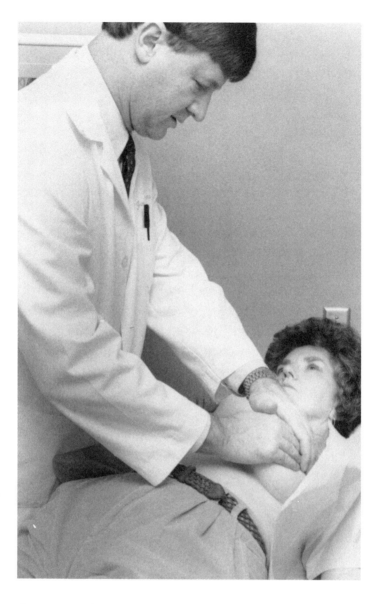

In screening for breast cancer, a physician examines a woman's breast for possible irregularities or growths.

izing in interpreting breast X rays) reads it. The radiologist carefully studies the X ray for unusual shadows, masses, distortions, unique patterns of tissue density, as well as any variations between the patient's two breasts.

Mammograms are given at various sites, including breast clinics, hospital radiology departments, mobile screening vans, and some doctor's offices. A doctor may schedule a mammogram for a patient, while in other instances the patient makes the appointment herself. The choice of where to have a mammogram is important, because these facilities can vary significantly. At mammography sites accredited by the American College of Radiology (ACR), the equipment, personnel, and procedures have been evaluated and approved. Doctors and technicians at accredited facilities are especially trained to perform and interpret breast X rays using machines that provide high-quality mammograms with a minimum of radiation exposure.

While at one time the ACR accreditation program was voluntary, the Mammography Quality Standards Act required that all mammography facilities be certified by the Secretary of Health and Human Services by October 1, 1994. The act mandates that facilities produce quality mammograms correctly read, interpret the X-ray films, and report the results to both the patients' doctor and the patient. The law also provides for data collection to determine accurately the effectiveness of U.S. breast cancer screening programs.

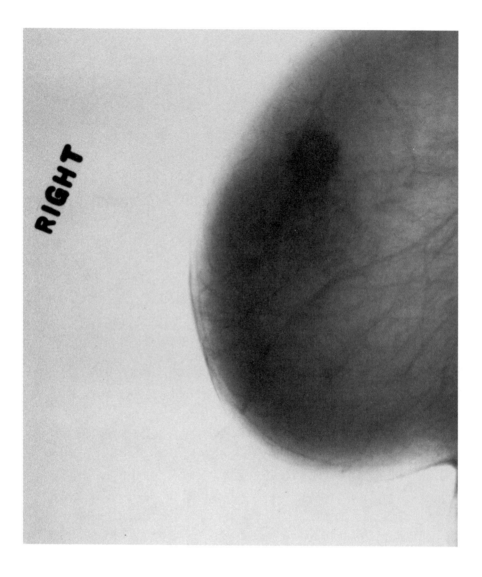

This mammogram of a woman's right breast reveals a malignancy. The tumor is indicated by the dark area in the upper portion of the breast.

ULTRASONOGRAPHY

This exam relies on high-frequency sound waves that enter the breast and bounce back, producing a picture called a sonogram, which is displayed on a screen. Sonograms can be useful in breast cancer detection, as they sometimes reveal whether a lump is a solid tissue mass or filled with fluid. Fluid-filled lumps are not cancerous, while a growth of solid tissue may or may not be malignant. Frequently mammograms are used in conjunction with sonograms.

COMPUTERIZED TOMOGRAPHY (CT SCANNING)

Here a computer assembles information from multiple X-ray views to devise a cross-sectional image of the breast. CT has been found to be especially useful in detecting breast lesions that don't show up well on either mammograms or sonograms, such as tumors extremely close to the chest wall.

POSSIBLE NEW BREAST CANCER DETECTION TECHNIQUES

Research is now being done on several techniques that may eventually be used in breast cancer detection. These include:

MAGNETIC RESPONSE IMAGING (MRI)

This procedure uses magnetic fields and radio waves to devise a likeness of body tissues.

POSITION EMISSION TOMOGRAPHY (PET SCANNING)
A scan for identifying abnormally active tissues.

LASER BEAM SCANNING
Here a strong laser beam is shined through the breast while a specialized camera on the breast's other side records the image.

SCINTIMAMMOGRAPHY
In this diagnostic procedure, a radioactive tracer is injected into the blood to identify malignancies in women with breast cancer. This experimental technique, which has been shown to be 90 percent effective, may eventually reduce the need for surgical biopsies.

TUMOR MARKERS
Tumor markers are chemical substances found in increased amounts in the blood of some cancer patients. Using specialized laboratory tests to identify elevated levels of certain tumor markers could prove helpful in breast cancer detection. Because many of these substances are naturally raised in some individuals, additional research is needed in this area.

MONITORING FOR GENETIC CHANGES
Someday it may be possible to identify women likely to develop breast cancer through specific genetic changes they experience.

In September 1994, medical research efforts headed by Mark Skolnick of the University of Utah and Roger Wiseman of the National Institute of Environmental Health Science in South Carolina announced that they had discovered and isolated a gene responsible for breast cancer. The gene, dubbed BRAC1, is only one of a number of genes linked to inherited forms of the disease, but it represents a vital breakthrough in our knowledge about all types of breast cancer. Researchers hope that as a result of this work, a genetic test will be devised enabling physicians to determine which of their patients are at risk of developing breast cancer from BRAC1. This would alert such women to be especially vigilant for the first signs of a tumor. Yet significantly more work is needed in this realm. Of all breast cancer cases diagnosed annually, just 5 to 10 percent are connected to an inherited gene, while BRAC1 is the culprit in only about half of these.

Presently, a physician may rely on a number of diagnostic techniques in determining that a woman is free of breast cancer. The doctor may continue to regularly monitor the patient, however, comparing these test results with future ones to note any changes in her breasts. In other instances, further procedures are required before the doctor can arrive at a diagnosis. These may include either type of the biopsies described below:

• Aspiration or needle biopsy. In this procedure a needle is used to withdraw either fluid or a tiny amount of tissue from a breast growth. The removed substance is sent to a lab to be analyzed.

This procedure frequently shows whether the lump is fluid-filled or a solid mass.

• Surgical biopsy. Here a doctor cuts out either all or a portion of a growth and any questionable surrounding tissue. A pathologist (a specialist in identifying diseases through the study of cells) examines the removed tissue under a microscope to determine if it's malignant.

Although early detection increases a woman's chances for survival, many women choose not to think about breast cancer. Besides failing to perform breast self-examination monthly, they'll avoid getting mammograms, pay no attention to small lumps that appear in their breasts, and fail to seek a second opinion if their family physician assures them that they need not be concerned about a growth. It's almost as if their anxiety over breast cancer helps to bring about their worst fear.

A case in point might be that of Martha McGregor (name changed). On July 10, 1988, at 3:18 A.M., sixty-three-year-old Martha McGregor died of breast cancer alone in a hospital. When the nurse had stopped in at midnight to check on her, the failing woman unnerved the health care professional by asking that she come back later, as the patient felt she wouldn't make it through the night. To the sorrow of her family, friends, and all those whose lives she touched, Martha McGregor's final premonition had been correct.

It was difficult for many to believe that Martha McGregor was gone. As a former hospital social worker and a busy wife and mother of three, she'd always been an active, seemingly healthy woman. And, although she might not have wanted to face it, Martha McGregor had been a prime candidate for breast cancer. She was more than forty years of age and had a sister who'd had cancer in both breasts.

After finding a small tumor near the nipple of her right breast, her longtime family physician told her not to be concerned. He said they'd keep an eye on the tiny lump to see if it grew or otherwise changed. Unfortunately, crucial years were lost through this "wait and see" approach as the later-discovered cancer coursed through Martha McGregor's body. Although the American Cancer Society recommends that women over fifty have mammograms annually, three years passed before Martha had one to further investigate the growth that had begun to look troublesome.

Some may be baffled at why an informed woman employed in a hospital, such as Martha McGregor, did not act earlier despite her doctor's hesitancy. Yet countless knowledgeable women continue to delay having mammograms that in some cases could mean the difference between life and death. Possibly the reason has to do with the nature of the disease. Martha McGregor's son thought he might have come across a plausible explanation for the widespread reluctance in an editorial appearing in *The Journal of the National Cancer Institute*, which read:

> *Surveys continue to document women's widespread lack of willingness to comply [with recommendations on breast self-examination]. Their*

reluctance is not surprising. We are asking women to try regularly to locate something in their bodies that will result in some degree of mutilation. We are asking women to try to find cancer in themselves.[7]

These sentiments were echoed by Dr. Susan Love, who noted, "The breast has some special psychological baggage—for one thing, there are all these associations with breast-feeding and nurturing the next generation. Then too, the breast is the most obvious identifying feature of femaleness. Think about it: if some androgynous-looking person comes walking down the street, the first thing you do to try to figure out if they're male or female is look at their chest."[8]

Perhaps Martha McGregor's reluctance to face the lump in her breast was best evidenced by her hesitancy to discuss it. She rarely spoke with her husband about the possibility of a malignancy. He recalled that when she first told him about the growth, "she didn't want to appear disturbed about it. She didn't express any fear or apprehension. She just didn't seem that concerned."[9] As a result of her attitude, her husband tended not to be as worried as he might normally have been.

In any case, once Martha McGregor finally had a mammogram, in June 1983, there seemed nothing to fear. The doctor checking the X rays had described her breasts as "normal." But the following day a radiologist reviewing the test discovered "a small curvilinear-shaped area of increased intensity." A little more than a month later, in an operation that took about twenty-three minutes, a local surgeon removed the troublesome lump. Martha McGregor assured her son that the growth had been benign and that she'd be fine. He didn't find out for months that she'd lied to him.

Unfortunately, the growth in Martha McGregor's right breast was cancerous. Her health outlook further diminished after the surgeon subsequently discovered a second firm mass in her left breast, along with lymph-node swelling. Soon afterward she had a mastectomy of her right breast and a biopsy of the left, with disconcerting results. Martha McGregor's cancer hadn't merely spread from one breast to another; she'd developed two distinct breast cancers, and the disease had already reached four lymph nodes on her left side. Several days later a mastectomy of her left breast was performed, leaving the surgeon concerned that the disease's spread might be even more extensive than they'd originally estimated.

Much later her son learned that his mother's surgeon had not been very optimistic about her future. The doctor wrote of Martha McGregor's prospects, "Due to her axillary metastatic involvement and the bilateral chest disease, she is certainly at high risk for recurrence. Her prognosis is therefore guarded."[10] But she never shared this information with her family. Instead, Martha McGregor put on a brave exterior and told them that she had an 85 percent chance for a "complete recovery and total remission."

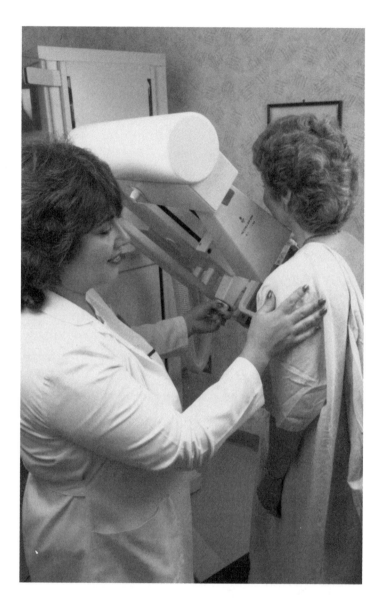

Here a woman is given a mammogram. Through mammography, small lumps, such as the one Martha McGregor found, are often detected at an early stage.

The next few months were devoted to various efforts to enhance Martha's survival chances. She endured twenty-five radiation treatments to her chest wall, along with eight courses of chemotherapy. The radiation therapy left her exhausted, while nausea, vomiting, and weakness followed each dose of chemotherapy. Yet through it all Martha McGregor continued to assure her family that she was winning the battle against cancer, and those close to her jokingly said that years from now she'd probably die from heart disease.

Reality came crashing through on February 26, 1985, however, when after experiencing a pain in her right leg, Martha McGregor's oncologist ordered a bone scan. Sadly, following seventeen months of her being seemingly cancer free, the breast cancer had spread to her bones. As the scan report indicated, "There are multiple sites of abnormal activity not present previously. They involve left fourth, fifth, and seventh posterior ribs, both pelvic bones, left parietal (skull) region, and several sites in the lower thoracic and lumbar spine ... . the appearance is compatible with metastatic disease."[11]

At that point the cancer seemed uncontainable. Martha McGregor's doctor started her on the anti-cancer drug tamoxifen, but before long she began experiencing severe pain in her hips, neck, back, and shoulders because of the cancer's invasive spread. It became increasingly difficult for her to walk, and by January 1988, her X rays and scans revealed that the cancer was rapidly moving through her skull and skeleton. Her doctor continued to treat her with a variety of drugs, but the cancer took it's brutal toll on her body. Martha McGregor still claimed that she'd beaten the odds even though her physicians were surprised that she'd survived this long.

By the last few months of Martha McGregor's life, it was clear to those around her that there wasn't much time left. She flew to California to visit her son and see her first grandchild. Her son was taken aback when he picked up his parents at the airport and saw how thin and drawn his now-limping mother had become. Although Martha fell in love instantly with her three-month-old grandson, her condition even made it physically painful for her to hold him.

While in California she did a videotaped interview with a friend of her son's who produced family histories. In it she said she hadn't wanted to "be a whining, complaining wife and mother. . . . I don't want my children to remember me that way. . . . I want my children to remember me as an active, useful human being. And that's why I've struggled for so long. I'm not afraid of death. But I'm afraid of dying if it's going to be a slow, painful, elongated thing. . . . And then I began to think in terms of mortality. And I just had to work that through. I don't like the idea of the world going on without me."[12]

Once Martha McGregor returned home, her doctors discovered that the cancer had spread to her lungs and liver. As the disease progressed, the woman's kidneys began to fail. Several days later she entered the hospital. In a call to their son, her husband reported in a barely audible voice, "The cancer is everywhere."[13] Nothing more needed to be said. At that point, the family knew that the woman they loved would not be coming home this time.

In assessing his mother's fate, her son needed to explore the reasons behind her death. There were pressing questions to which he wanted answers. Why hadn't preventive health measures been practiced, and why was there a significant time lapse between the detection and treatment of his mother's disease? Given her age and medical background, his mother should have had a mammogram each year. Yet this had hardly been the case. Despite indicating on her medical history form that her sister had breast cancer, there was nothing in her physician's records to show that he'd advised her to have annual mammograms. Her husband was also unable to recall his wife ever saying that her doctor suggested it.

Martha McGregor's son concluded that his mother's physician failed to adequately keep abreast of the recommendations of major cancer organizations regarding mammography. This is not as unusual as it may seem. A 1990 nationwide study revealed that only 37 percent of physicians faithfully follow such guidelines, while in three other major studies, doctors admitted that they forgot to encourage their age-appropriate female patients to have annual mammograms. In other instances, physicians assume that another doctor has already told the patient to have a mammogram, while there's also speculation that a number of doctors remain unconvinced that mammograms actually save lives. Professional jealousy and rivalry between radiologists and other physicians has been cited as another causal factor.

Yet it's still not certain that additional mammograms would have saved Martha McGregor's life. Possibly the mammogram she had in 1983 did not pick up the lump in her left breast that eventually wreaked havoc on her body. It's not uncommon, even for mammograms done at some of the most respected medical institutions, to occasionally yield incorrect "negative" readings, thus providing the patient with a false sense of security.

In some cases, the likelihood of receiving an incorrect mammogram reading is further compounded by incompetence on the part of a small number of physicians. That's what happened in New York in June 1994, when, after receiving a complaint from a surgeon regarding a flawed mammogram, the New York City Health Department seized more than one hundred mammogram results and deactivated the mammography equipment at the offices of two physicians. Court transcripts revealed that one of the doctors had been previously cited for mammogram infractions and that his mammography equipment had been sealed on three other occasions. The records further indicated that the physician in question had a history of noncompliance with quality assurance and safety standards regarding mammograms.

As for Martha McGregor, her son eventually concluded that her doctor's laxness was only part of a broader problem. As he wrote:

> *[Her] decline and death were the fault of many. [Her doctor for gross neglect of a patient] who believed in him; the medical community, for caring less about women's health than men's; the media, for sharing in that twisted priority; my father, for not pushing harder when he knew of her lump; me, for not prodding her with my usual reporter's skepticism about authority. But ultimately the blame lies with my mother. . . . [She trusted] the men in the white coats, the men with medical degrees. She trusted them to take care of her when she, above all needed to take care of herself.*[14]

Martha McGregor has not been forgotten by the many people who so enjoyed her warmth, kindness, and spirit. The frightening finality imposed by the deadly illness that claimed her life remains with them as well. As her son concluded, "her genetic legacy, along with her sister's, places both her daughters and her niece at higher risk of suffering the disease themselves. Each has lumps. Each is terrified."[15] Unfortunately, at this time, millions of women worldwide share their dread.

2

TREATMENT

I lost an old friend. That's how I refer to my mastectomy. But that was twenty-two years ago. Just after surgery, I held a news conference and got the word out telling women not to be afraid. I was the first celebrity to go public with her breast cancer. I felt that I could help my sisters.[1]

— *Shirley Temple Black, diplomat, former actress*

Being diagnosed with breast cancer is always unnerving, even if the woman has suspected that she has the illness. Yet despite the distress in receiving this unsettling news, it's crucial that a newly diagnosed patient learn as much as possible about her condition and the available treatment options. The doctors can tell whether the cancer began in the breast's ducts or lobules and may also be able to determine if it's invasive (has, or will, spread to sur-rounding breast tissue). At this juncture, specialized tests may be conducted to determine if the cancer is likely to grow slowly or quickly and if the disease may respond to hormones during the treatment phase.

Often treatment begins a few weeks after diag-nosis. Ideally, by then the patient will have acquainted herself with the particulars of her situa-tion, gotten a second medical opinion, and begun to prepare herself, her family, and involved friends for what's ahead. The patient is likely to have many questions. Besides wanting to learn what her chances for survival and recovery are, she may also want to know how she'll look after treatment and to what degree her lifestyle and daily regime will be altered in the months to come.

Breast cancer may be treated in a variety of ways, depending on, among other factors, the size and location of the tumor, whether or not the can-cer has spread, the woman's age and general health, and her personal preferences.

Cancer treatments are either local or systemic. Local treatments, such as surgery and radiation, are methods used to remove, destroy, or control cancer cells in a specifically defined area of the body. On the other hand, systemic treatments, such as chemotherapy and hormone therapy, attack or control cancer cells throughout the body. Some patients may have only one form of treat-ment: others require a combination of both. The different ways breast cancer is treated are described below.

SURGERY

Surgery remains the most commonly used treatment in fighting breast cancer. Among the available surgical options is "breast-sparing surgery," or lumpectomy, in which the goal is to remove the cancer without losing the breast. In a lumpectomy, only the malignant tumor and a small amount of healthy tissue surrounding it is cut out.

On the other hand, the various forms of a more extensive operation known as mastectomy entails both cutting away the malignant tumor along with either part or all of the woman's breast and the surrounding area. In a partial or segmental mastectomy, the surgeon removes the cancerous growth and a portion of the breast tissue around it, as well as the lining covering the chest muscles beneath the tumor. With a total, or simple, mastectomy, the entire breast is removed; a modified radical mastectomy involves cutting away the breast, a portion of the lymph nodes beneath the arm, and the lining covering the chest muscles. In some instances the procedure may also include removal of the smaller of the two chest muscles. The most inclusive type of mastectomy is known as a radical mastectomy, or the Halsted radical mastectomy. In this extreme procedure, the woman's breast, chest muscles, and all the lymph nodes beneath her arm, as well as some healthy skin and fat, is surgically removed.

SIDE EFFECTS OF BREAST SURGERY

Breast removal can cause the patient's weight to shift, thereby affecting her balance. This shift in balance could result in further discomfort in the back and neck area. Following breast removal, the patient's skin in that part of her body may be tight, while it's likely that her arm and shoulder muscles on that side may be stiff and sore. Many postmastectomy women also temporarily lose strength and have limited movement in these muscles, although for only a small number of patients is the strength loss permanent. After a mastectomy, patients may experience numbness and tingling in the chest, underarm, arm, and shoulders because of nerves being injured or cut during the procedure. These sensations may continue for several weeks after the operation, but in some instances the numbness remains.

When the lymph nodes are removed during breast surgery, the flow of lymph (the colorless liquid of the lymphatic system that carries cells that help fight infection and disease) is slowed. The subsequent buildup of lymph in the arm and hand can result in swelling (lymphedema). Lymph node removal also makes it more difficult for the body to combat arm and hand infections on that side. Therefore, in these instances the woman should ask her doctor how to handle any cuts, scratches, or insect bites in that area of her body.

While the radical mastectomy was almost exclusively used to treat breast cancer for about a hundred years until 1970, it is not regularly resorted to today. Over time the medical profession learned more about how cancer spreads and determined that for the most part this surgery was excessive for patients with early breast cancer. In fact, studies revealed that women who had only the affected breast tissue and lymph nodes removed survived as frequently as women undergoing the most extensive and cosmetically devastating procedure. As noted by Dr. David W. Kline of Columbia-Presbyterian Hospital in New York City, "Breast conservation treatment—lumpectomy, dissection of the nodes and radiation—gives a cure rate equal to mastectomy."[2] Some physicians also believe that retaining the breast may help maintain the immune system and serve as a buffer, because in instances of a reoccurrence, women who've had mastectomies often don't fare as well as do women who've had lumpectomies.

Given these factors, lumpectomy might be thought to have become the more common mode for treating breast cancer—yet surprisingly, it is not. A jointly conducted survey by the National Cancer Institute and the American Cancer Society revealed that in 1986, a year after national clinical trials indicating that a lumpectomy plus radiation is an appropriate early breast cancer treatment, of the 37,000 women treated for the disease, only 12 percent had lumpectomies, while 88 percent underwent more disfiguring operations.

Actually a number of factors, besides the medical aspects of her case, may determine the type of treatment a woman with breast cancer receives.

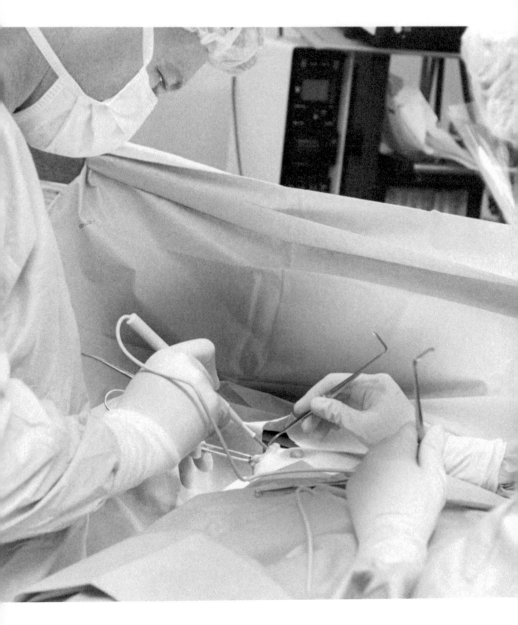

The breast cancer surgery performed here could be instrumental in saving this woman's life.

According to Dr. Beryl McCormick, radiation oncologist at Memorial Sloan-Kettering Cancer Care Center, "Women sometimes choose whether they'll have a mastectomy or lumpectomy plus radiation based on the first doctor visit. Those seeing an older male surgeon may be told, 'If you were my wife . . .' "[3] It's not uncommon for the treating physician's attitudes and beliefs to influence his or her recommended treatment choices. For example, some people feel that surgeons often favor extensive surgery over the other possible treatment options.

There may also be a tendency on the physician's part to go with the procedure he or she is accustomed to. Breast cancer specialist Dr. Susan Love remarked, "Another problem is that most surgeons are more comfortable performing a mastectomy than a lumpectomy, and since the two treatments are equal in their success at saving lives, of course they're inclined to recommend the one they're more comfortable with."[4] Dr. Love continued, "Even when a patient has gotten over the shock of diagnosis, doctors can make it hard for her to come to a good, clearheaded decision about what kind of surgery she wants. They'll say things like, 'Well, you're elderly and you're widowed—you don't need your breast anymore. Why don't you just have a mastectomy? It'll be easier.' In my experience, though, older women aren't any more likely than younger ones to want a mastectomy."[5] These sentiments were underscored by two recent studies confirming that older breast cancer patients often receive less desirable treatment than do their younger counterparts, despite the fact that a woman's risk for breast cancer increases with age.[6]

Dr. Love further stressed that the individual physician's surgical skills also influence how he or she might sway a breast cancer patient. She stated, "To do a good lumpectomy is simply more difficult. On top of that, most breast surgeons have never been trained in it, because it's a relatively new operation and they went to medical schools in the days when everyone just did mastectomies."[7]

Still another factor determining the type of treatment a breast cancer patient receives is her place of residence. Despite ample evidence supporting the effectiveness of lumpectomy as an option for early breast cancer patients, in many parts of the country mastectomy, nevertheless, remains the dominant procedure. Studies reveal that the greatest number of lumpectomies are performed in the northeast, while the southwest has the lowest rate. The data further indicate that the majority of patients receiving lumpectomies were white females residing in urban areas. These women frequently had their surgery in teaching hospitals or facilities affiliated with medical schools in which adequate equipment for the necessary follow-up radiation therapy was available. It may be significant that the seventeen states that have informed-consent laws—requiring physicians to acquaint patients with various available treatment options—are the ones in which lumpectomies, or breast conservation treatment (BCT), are most common.

RADIATION

Radiation therapy (also known as radiotherapy), which can either be administered externally or internally, uses high-energy rays to damage cancer cells and stop their spread. A patient being treated with radiation externally has the rays targeted at the problem area from a machine outside of her body. These patients live at home and go to a hospital or clinic each day for the procedure. If their radiation therapy follows a lumpectomy, many patients will receive ongoing treatments five days a week for five to six weeks. At the end of their therapy, some patients may be given an additional boost of radiation at the tumor site. With internal radiation treatments, implants of radioactive material encased in plastic tubes are placed directly within the breast. Patients receiving this type of radiation therapy remain hospitalized while being treated.

SIDE EFFECTS

Among the most common side effects of radiation are exhaustion, as well as red, dry, tender, and itchy skin in the area treated. Toward the later part of treatment, the patient may feel especially drained and tired and the skin area targeted may become somewhat moist. The side effects of radiation ther-

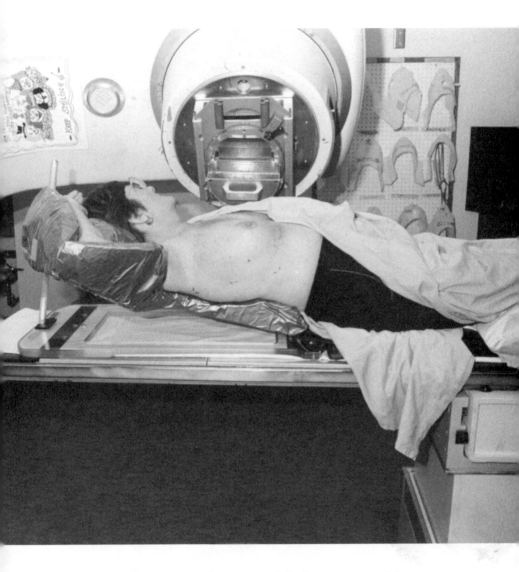

This woman is being treated for breast cancer with external radiation therapy. Often used in conjunction with surgery, radiation treatments can either shrink a tumor before it's surgically removed or destroy any cancer cells remaining after the operation.

apy, however, are temporary and disappear following treatment.

CHEMOTHERAPY

Chemotherapy involves the use of drugs to destroy cancer cells. Breast cancer patients undergoing chemotherapy will usually be given a combination of medications either taken orally or injected into the woman's arm muscle. Chemotherapy is generally administered in cycles. Following a treatment period, the patient is given a recovery time prior to beginning the next cycle. Although the majority of breast cancer patients receive chemotherapy as hospital outpatients, at a doctor's office, or at home, some women need to remain hospitalized during treatment.

SIDE EFFECTS
Chemotherapy's side effects vary with the different drugs that may be used. The anticancer drugs in chemotherapy tend to affect rapidly dividing cells, but unfortunately, besides attacking malignant cells, the medication also acts similarly on such rapidly dividing cells as blood cells (cells that carry oxygen throughout the body, fight infection, and cause blood to clot), hair follicle cells, and cells lining the digestive track. As the chemotherapy affects the patient's blood cells, she may feel increasingly tired and become more prone to infections, as well as bruise and bleed more easily. The drugs' effect on other healthy cells can cause the patient's hair to

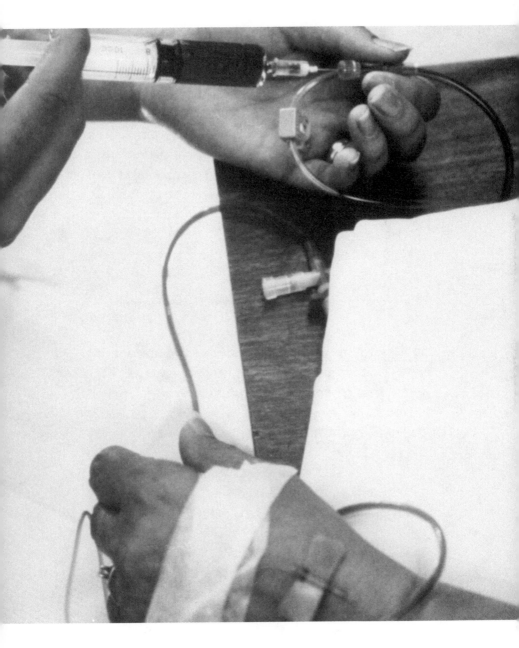

*A cancer patient on chemotherapy is injected with a
combination of drugs designed to destroy cancer cells.*

fall out, and she may experience a loss of appetite, nausea, vomiting, and mouth sores. These side effects are temporary and will pass once the treatment is over.

At times, anticancer drugs may also damage a woman's ovaries. If as a result of treatment the ovaries fail to produce hormones, a patient may experience such menopausal symptoms as hot flashes, vaginal dryness, and irregular periods. Some women become infertile, and in patients over thirty-five or forty years of age, these side effects may be permanent.

HORMONE THERAPY

Hormone therapy involves the use of hormones to curtail cancer-cell growth. With breast cancer, hormone therapy may entail using drugs to alter hormone functioning or surgically removing the patient's ovaries which produce hormones.

SIDE EFFECTS

Hormone therapy's side effects depend on the nature of the treatment or the specific drug used. A young woman who has her ovaries removed for this purpose will immediately experience menopause. In these cases, the typical menopausal symptoms such as hot flashes and vaginal dryness tend to be more severe.

Tamoxifen, a medication proported to reduce breast cancer recurrences by about 30 percent, is frequently used when drugs are employed in hormone therapy. Although tamoxifen does not stop the production of the hormone estrogen, it blocks the body's use of it.

Tamoxifen's side effects are less potent than those of ovary removal. The woman may experience vaginal dryness and hot flashes but not menopause or infertility. The drug's critics argue, however, that despite its effectiveness in combating breast cancer, tamoxifen poses serious risks of its own. There have been documented cases of eye damage, liver failure, and cancer of the uterine lining among some of its users.

Tamoxifen, a medication used to fight breast cancer, blocks the body's use of the hormone estrogen.

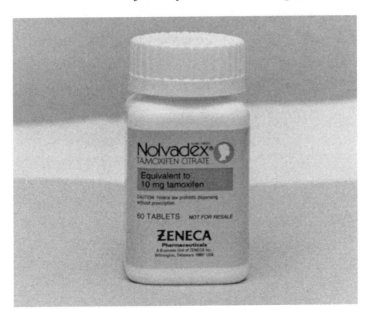

POSSIBLE NEW TREATMENTS

In addition to the traditional methods of fighting breast cancer, scientists are also striving to find new ways to fight the disease. Initially, promising procedures are tested and refined through clinical trials. In these studies on volunteer patients, a new approach is compared with a standard treatment to evaluate its efficiency and safety. While in some instances there may be an element of risk involved with a not-yet-approved procedure, on the other hand, these participants may be the first to profit from an innovative, possibly lifesaving measure.

At present, a variety of treatments—including new ways to combine some existing anticancer treatments—are being explored for patients in all stages of breast cancer. A number of projects have centered on learning if extremely high doses of anticancer drugs are more beneficial in destroying breast cancer cells than the dosages currently used. Because large quantities of these medications gravely damage the patient's bone marrow (the spongy material in some bones in which blood cells are produced), scientists are also searching for an effective means to counteract this effect. Among these are bone-marrow transplants and colony-stimulating factors where laboratory-made substances much like those found in the human body are used to stimulate the production of blood cells.

There have also been some promising developments in biological-therapy, or immuno-therapy, that employ various substances to boost the patient's immune system's response to cancer. More than twenty-five different agents are now being studied to determine if they provoke immune responses to defeat breast cancer as well as other cancers.

There's a great deal of excitement over advances in gene research, as well. While just a small percent of breast cancer is hereditary, and therefore caused by a particular gene, there's growing evidence that genes play an important role in breast cancer in another way. Some researchers think that outside factors such as diet or certain environmental pollutants could alter specific genes in the body in such a manner as to promote cancer. Once scientists know more about how and why this happens, they might be able to devise some form of gene therapy to correct the problem. Many cancer researchers are extremely enthusiastic over this and similar potentially lifesaving prospects. As Michael Sporn, former director of a new National Cancer Center Institute lab, optimistically predicted, "Over the next twenty-five years, breast cancer will disappear like the Cheshire Cat."[8]

Still, at this time, the outlook for women with breast cancer is not as rosy. Regardless of the type of therapy administered, being treated for cancer often entails unpleasant physical side effects as well as draining emotional upheavals. Some breast cancer patients believe the medical establishment must heighten its sensitivity to the feelings of patients facing such a potentially disfiguring or even fatal illness. They've argued that at times breast cancer patients have been dealt with more like assembly-line products than thinking, feeling human beings.

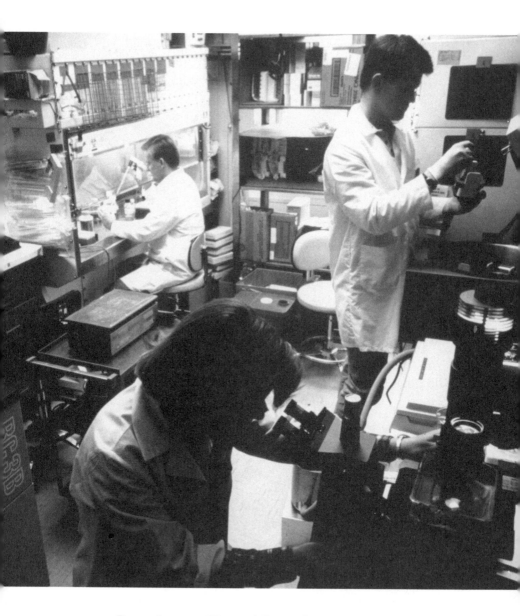

Researchers at a National Cancer Institute lab continue
the search for breast cancer's causes as well as new ways
to arrest the disease.

In any case, that's how Joleen Lasker [name changed] regarded her experience. At first everyone told Joleen how fortunate she was. Although at just thirty-five she'd been diagnosed with breast cancer, the disease had been detected at an early stage, allowing her surgeon to remove the lump while leaving Joleen's breast intact. The young woman's lumpectomy was followed by radiation treatments, but despite having avoided some of the more traumatic consequences of breast cancer, Joleen still underwent a grueling ordeal.

Shortly after her diagnosis, Joleen Lasker landed in the hands of an oncologist, or cancer specialist. She had a hint of things to come when she entered his office for the first time and the nurse offered the greeting, "New patient? Give me your insurance card!" That was how Joleen's battle with breast cancer began. A war choreographed for the most part by health care professionals whom she described as handling breast cancer patients "like airline baggage: checked in, weighed, X-rayed, tagged, thrown on a conveyor belt, and forgotten about unless it gets lost."[9]

Among her most unsettling experiences were the radiation treatments that she described this way:

"Don't move," barked the X-ray technician as I lay shaking, half-naked in a dark room decorated with DANGER HIGH RADIATION AREA *signs. I winced as the radiation therapist unsheathed a heavy navy-blue Magic Marker,*

casually drew what looked like a flowchart across my chest, and ordered me not to remove it until the end of treatment. I felt as if I'd been raped by a felt-tip pen. Every morning I endured the indignity of having my marks "freshened" as if I were a football field being rechalked. Yet nobody even seemed aware that this process was dehumanizing. "It could be worse," I was reminded. "In some clinics, you get tattooed."[10]

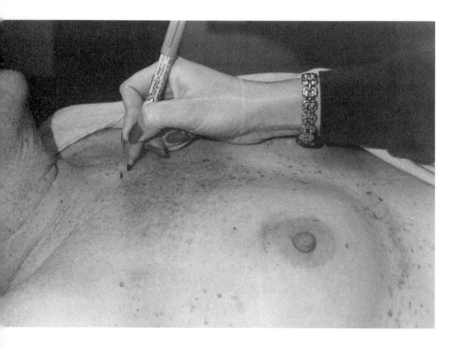

A patient's breast is "marked" for radiation therapy so that high energy rays can be targeted at a specific cancer cell cluster. These treatments damage malignant cells to prevent them from multiplying within the body.

Joleen added that, while she was advised to see an internist, surgeon, oncologist, and radiation therapist in dealing with her breast cancer, at no time was it suggested that she seek the services of a mental health professional to assist her with the psychological repercussions of the disease. Lasker eventually found a psychologist who was extremely helpful; ironically, these sessions were the only part of her breast cancer treatment not covered by Joleen's health insurance policy.

Some think the emotional aspects of breast cancer are frequently ignored by the medical community because the illness is one that largely affects women. At times, breast cancer patients desiring counseling have forgone it because they didn't want to seem needy or incapable of handling the disease's impact. This was especially true for breast cancer patient Jane Greer [name changed], a physician's wife who described how she was treated as follows:

> *I kept saying, "Maybe I need to see a therapist." But all my doctors said, 'Oh, no, you don't need one.' They kept insisting that I was doing fine. How did they know if I was doing fine? I think it was their way of telling me to shut up. . . . I guess to them it's no different than having a cavity. The dentist doesn't suggest a therapist.*[11]

Of course, tooth decay isn't potentially fatal.

3

PRECAUTIONS AGAINST BREAST CANCER

I want to put out the message that life does go on. Following my second mastectomy in 1984, I took tamoxifen for over two years. Since then I've been treatment-free. I don't feel like I'm living under a cloud. Worrying about it doesn't prevent it. I just feel grateful and lucky.[1]

—Phyllis Newman, Broadway actress

Unlike some breast cancer patients, Crystal Stanza [name changed] had a warm and trusting relationship with her physician. Yet the day he told her he was concerned about her last mammogram, she felt he was either mistaken or had her X rays confused with another patient's.

Having breast cancer was not a possibility Crystal felt ready to face. But her doctor refused to let her remain in denial and insisted that she immediately see a breast surgeon for a biopsy. When

Crystal called the surgeon's office, she learned that her doctor had called ahead and that she was to come in that afternoon. Only hours had passed, but it was becoming increasingly harder to believe that nothing was wrong.

The surgeon examined her mammogram and described the various possibilities. Then, following a pause, he told her that after twenty-five years in the field, he knew that tumors like hers are usually malignant. There was no hiding from it now; the truth had come pounding on her front door.

She thought about how she'd tell Brian, her husband. This was her second marriage, and the couple had been married only eleven weeks. Crystal remembered the words she said at their wedding ceremony—they'd vowed to love one another "in sickness and in health," but she felt this had come too soon. Yet she knew there wasn't a right time to have breast cancer.

Crystal broke the news to Brian when he returned from work that evening. They cried and hugged one another, and Brian assured his new wife that they'd get through this together. But neither had an appetite for dinner that night, and they just let the telephone ring rather than answer it.

The next day, the breast surgeon met with both Crystal and her husband. He explained that if the tumor were as small as it appeared on the film, Crystal had the option of having either a lumpectomy or a modified radical mastectomy. Although the surgeon assured the couple that both operations had similar survival rates, Crystal chose the mastec-

Here a physician explains available
medical options to a couple.

tomy, as she and her husband were apprehensive about possibly having any disease left in her. She further decided to forgo breast reconstruction, as she didn't want to endure additional surgery. When the doctor asked Brian how he'd feel about having a wife with only one breast, he said he married Crystal because he wanted to spend the rest of his life with her, not because she had two breasts.

Once Crystal Stanza woke up in the recovery

room after the operation, she was relieved to hear that all had gone well. Following her mastectomy, she learned specific arm exercises to recover the full range of motion in her arm and shoulder. Luckily, Crystal's cancer did not return. When friends ask her what's new around the time she's had her annual mammogram, she's always been pleased to answer, "Nothing."

Tracey Samuelson, like Crystal Stanza, is another woman who wasn't "supposed" to have breast cancer. She was just twenty-nine when diagnosed, and the mother of four small children. Tracey found the lump in her breast herself, but her doctor had told her not to worry about it. He'd even predicted that the growth might become larger before going away.

Although Tracey Samuelson detected the lump when it was just the size of a pea, in less than six months it grew to about two centimeters in diameter. At that point she insisted that her physician remove it. As she recalled her decision and the surgery results:

> [I]t was so large, it was—it was unsightly. . . . So I wanted it removed regardless. But I was—I had been told it wasn't cancer. So when they took it out and they called me in and told me I had cancer, I thought, "But that's not possible. I was told I didn't have cancer."[2]

Unfortunately, Tracey Samuelson did not enjoy the complete recovery Crystal Stanza did. The cancer spread to her brain and she was told the disease was terminal. Even while she was still alive, Tracey sent her children to live with her mother-in-law, because having a malignant brain tumor made it impossible for her to care for them the way she'd like to, and she didn't know how much time she had left.

Breast cancer has become a major health concern for women across America. Its victims are rich and poor as well as young and old. It's the number-one cause of death for females between fifteen and fifty years of age and the leading killer of African-American women of all ages. Perhaps most frightening of all is that at present more than one million women in America have the disease but don't know it yet. Out of these, some, like Crystal Stanza, will have encouraging outcomes, while others will be forced to deal with the dim prognosis Tracey Samuelson faced.

Although physicians aren't certain why breast cancer is on the rise, there are some things women can do to help themselves in the fight against it. Listed below is a summary of some possibly lifesaving measures.

EARLY DETECTION

In dealing with breast cancer, early detection is of prime importance. It enhances the possibility of a complete recovery, and broadens the range of available treatment options as well. More than 95 percent of women whose breast cancers are confined

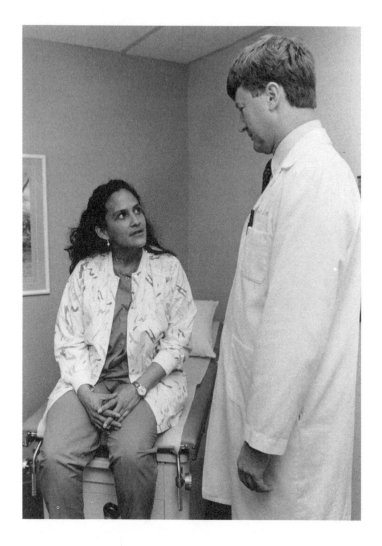

Research suggests that breast cancer, which has been shown to be particularly lethal among African-American females, strikes an unusually high number of these woman under the age of forty-five. That makes it especially important for African-American females to be aware of early detection measures.

to a single milk duct are still alive five years following treatment. The same is true for 85 percent of
the women whose malignancies measure less than
four-fifths of an inch in diameter. However, only 10
percent of the women whose breast cancers was left
untreated until the malignancy spread to distant
parts of their bodies are likely to survive for five
years.

Breast self-examination and regularly scheduled
mammograms for age-appropriate women are crucial aspects of early detection. In fact, the majority
of malignant tumors are accidently found by
women themselves. Frequently, women who regularly practice breast self-examination identify
growths at an early stage prior to the cancer's
spread.

DIET AND EXERCISE

As was mentioned in the section on risk factors in
Chapter 1, some evidence points to a connection
between breast cancer and a diet high in animal fat.
Although all the data isn't in yet, the National
Cancer Institute recommends that women limit the
fat content of their total daily caloric intake. It's
wise to substitute margarine for butter, select low-
fat diary products, and choose lean meats or substitute vegetable for meat dishes.

These recommendations are supported by studies conducted in Italy in which researchers inter-

viewed more than 250 women, including nearly every breast cancer patient in the Province of Vercelli. These women were compared to 499 cancer-free women that matched the first group in age and economic status. The scientists found that the females who consumed larger quantities of whole milk, high fat cheese, butter, and meat were more likely to have breast cancer. In fact, women with the highest intake of saturated fat or animal protein were two to three times more likely to develop breast cancer than were those with low-fat consumption. However, as the precise role of diet in breast cancer is still not entirely clear, more research is necessary.

Exercise may be helpful in lowering a women's risk for breast cancer as well. In a study conducted by Harvard reproductive biologist Rose Frisch and involving more than 5,000 female college graduates, athletic women were found to have at least a 35 percent lower level of breast cancer than those who didn't exercise. While this study didn't conclusively prove that exercise is a factor in breast cancer, numerous scientists suspect that this might be so. Further research done at both Harvard and at Rockefeller University in New York City indicates that athletes tend to have lower levels of a form of estrogen that may play a role in breast cancer.

The measures women can now take to guard against breast cancer may eventually be enhanced by the prevention research in which scientists are actively engaged. Among the areas being explored

*What's wrong with this picture? A low-fat dessert
would have been a better choice in helping this
woman to lower her risk for breast cancer.*

is that of dietary "chemoprevention." In Italy, where this technique is being tried, women who've been treated for breast cancer are given a synthetic form of vitamin A known as 4-PHR to prevent them from developing cancer in their other breast. Scientists in other areas are studying how vitamins C and E as well as beta-carotene (the form of vitamin A found in fruits and vegetables) may act to prevent breast cancer. Still other researchers are looking into how substances known as phytochemicals occurring naturally in many fruits, vegetables and some unusual edible plants may be extracted, purified, and used to supplement our diets as cancer preventatives.

Among the most drastic options in breast cancer prevention is prophylactic mastectomy, which entails the surgical removal of both breasts to prevent their developing malignant tumors. This option is sometimes chosen by women at extremely high risk for breast cancer, such as someone from a family in which every female has had the disease. The majority of women are counseled by their doctors against this extreme alternative, because the surgery is both physically and emotionally draining and in most cases breasts removed during this procedure have been shown to be cancer-free. Another drawback is that the operation often leaves behind a small amount of breast tissue in which malignant tumors can still develop.

Instead of prophylactic mastectomy, many physicians suggest that very high-risk patients have frequent clinical breast examinations and mammo-

The two women shown here work out at a gym.
A moderate but consistent level of exercise may
help to reduce the risk of breast cancer.

grams. A woman who still wants a prophylactic mastectomy because her concern over developing breast cancer undermines her quality of life should get a second medical opinion as well as take several months to consider her decision before undergoing the surgery.

4

THE POLITICS OF BREAST CANCER

*I no longer think of myself as a person with can-
cer, I've discovered something else growing in
me. I call it my voice, a voice that tells me who I
am and what I want to do. I first started hearing it after my breast cancer, in 1986.*[1]

—*Jill Eikenberry, actress*

Dateline ... Washington, D.C.

The scene is a political action rally on a steamy hot
summer Sunday. About seven thousand demonstra-
tors have come to the country's capital to raise funds
for the fight against breast cancer. These activists
hope to raise the consciousness of both the lawmak-
ers and the nation at large. Many have traded their
usual fashion accessories for buttons, t-shirts, and
signs bearing slogans such as, SILENT NO MORE
and THE WIFE YOU SAVE MAY BE YOUR
OWN.

At a gathering sponsored by the National Breast Cancer Coalition, the words of those addressing the crowd from the podium are unapologetic and often riveting. Thirty-seven-year-old Sherry Kohlenberg of Virginia, a veteran in the war against breast cancer, is among the speakers. As she walks to the platform, it is obvious that the disease had taken its toll on her body. She looks thin and her hat shifts on her head because of hair loss resulting from chemotherapy. Yet she seems undaunted as she defiantly states:

> *This year 46,000 women will die of breast cancer. I will probably be among those statistics. I will leave behind my husband and partner of eighteen years, a motherless child, a devastated family and too many friends. I will not get to watch my son grow up, or grow old with my husband. And the worst part is that I am not alone. This family tragedy happens every time a new diagnosis is made, and every time a woman's life is stolen by breast cancer."[2]*

She stresses that though there's often a backlash when women speak out, she will continue to say what needs to be said for as long as she is able to. "I will not go silently," Kohlenberg warns. "I will go shouting into that dark night: Enough is enough." A friend standing nearby comments, "She's dying and she knows it."[3] Pointing at the Capitol Building, the friend adds, "We've gotten in those people's faces, and we're going to stay there."[4]

While breast cancer political-action groups have become increasingly visible in recent years, some feel that the movement actually had its start in the early 1970s when prominent American women began to publicly reveal that they had breast cancer. Previously, breast cancer victims tended to remain "in the closet," hiding a disease that many believed could rob them of their femininity and eventually their lives. Yet much of the stigma associated with the disease began to dissolve when, in 1972, former child star Shirley Temple Black went public with her personal battle against the disease. Two years later, First Lady Betty Ford disclosed that she'd had breast cancer, while shortly thereafter the vice president's wife, Happy Rockefeller, announced that she was going through the same ordeal. The issue was readily discussed by 1976, when news reporter Betty Rollins wrote the best-selling book, *First You Cry*, detailing her fight to survive breast cancer. More than a decade later, after learning she needed a biopsy, First Lady Nancy Reagan told the nation, "I guess it's my turn."[5]

With the reality of this devastating disease in the open, women sought out others who'd shared their unique spectrum of experiences. This broad-based unification provided these women with a much-needed well of support and information in addition to a springboard for future political action. Taking their lead from AIDS activists of the 1980s, breast cancer support groups combined their energy and efforts to form a national political advocacy movement. Today there are a wide range of breast cancer political action groups united under the umbrella of the National Breast Cancer Coalition, founded in 1991. Within a year of its beginning, 150 groups had banded together. The number soon rose to 190 and continues to grow.

As one member described the phenomenon, "The AIDS activists were our model. They showed that if the populace became very concerned, then the politicians would respond."[6] Many of the women were new to the realm of protests and activism. But, fueled by their rage over their often overlooked plight and the insinuation by scientists and politicians that the disease is under control, they were determined to become a moving and potent voice for the many thousands of women they represent.

Breast cancer activists want more than just increased research funding; they also want more studies on the underlying causes of the disease, which would entail a shift from the present focus on early detection and treatment. Many are discouraged by the usual, limited treatment options of surgery, radiation, and chemotherapy, or as breast cancer specialist Dr. Susan Love termed it, "slash, burn, and poison."[7] Love argues, "Early detection is not early enough. . . . We have to be the voice, the obnoxious voice. We can't shut up now."[8] Love further stressed that cancer found on a mammogram may have already been there for six to eight years—while the cancer usually has access to the bloodstream by the third year, allow-

Breast cancer advocates at a 1994 California rally
organize to garner support for their cause.

ing a malignancy to spread prior to detection. Although some women's immune systems defeat the escaping cancer cells, in others these cells eventually reach other organs where they grow sufficiently large in number to threaten the woman's survival.

Why hasn't the medical establishment previously directed more research toward learning the precise causes of breast cancer? The answer may actually be more insidious than might readily be believed. As Dr. Devra Lee Davis, Ph.D., M.P.H., cited when testifying in December 1991 at a congressional hearing on breast cancer:

One may speculate about why so little attention has been paid to efforts to prevent a disease that afflicts so many women, but the fact of this deficit remains glaringly clear. Prevention is less glamorous than treatment and few profit financially if it succeeds."[9]

Dr. Davis believes the war against breast cancer is largely being waged on the wrong front. At the hearing, she stressed that more time and money needs to be focused on such factors as diet; prolonged high-dose hormone therapy; the effects of alcohol, stress, and exercise; as well as exposure to pesticides and other synthetic organic chemicals that concentrate in the body's fatty tissues.

The redirection of breast cancer research was also advocated by still another breast cancer medical expert, who testified,

We have gotten the maximum effect from the traditional treatments of surgery, radiation, and chemotherapy and need to go beyond them into new and innovative modes of treatment. We need to invest our dollars in promising new leads in tumor genetics and immunology, and not just new ways of giving chemotherapy.[10]

So far the coalition women have been extremely successful fund-raisers. In its first year the coalition increased national funds for breast cancer research by nearly 50 percent securing a $43 million increase. The following year, the women raised an astounding $300 million more.

Often, their power has sprung from largely grass-roots sources. In a 1992 drive, the women hoped to deliver 175,000 signatures to officials in Washington, D.C., one signature for every woman likely to be stricken with breast cancer that year. And by the time October (Breast Cancer Awareness Month) arrived, they left for the capital with an impressive 600,000 signatures instead.

A key element in their overall success was securing the support of Iowa Democratic Senator Tom Harkin. Harkin, who lost two sisters to breast cancer, tied money for increased funding to an allotment for the Defense Department. In 1992, the army budgeted $25 million to screen and treat the thousands of enlisted women for breast cancer. Harkin further proposed that the army's $25 million health budget be increased to $210 million and that the additional funds be earmarked for breast cancer research.

When the bill was voted on in the Senate, quite a few elected officials formerly opposed to increased funding for breast cancer research hurriedly changed their opinions and votes. A lobbyist for the National Breast Cancer Coalition described what occurred: "In the Year of the Woman [1992] they didn't dare go back and tell their constituents that they had voted against this successful strategy."[11] Although only 51 votes were needed, the bill passed 87 to 4.

Besides increased funding for breast cancer research, the National Breast Cancer Coalition wants breast cancer screening to be available for all women as well as a comprehensive national strategy for dealing with this disease. The activists believe this is essential for all women. According to Fran Visco, a Philadelphia lawyer and Coalition officer, "The problem now is that there are isolated pockets of people looking at breast cancer, and no one is talking to anyone else. These turf battles are fought and we lose."[12]

At times, formulating a cohesive national policy on breast cancer and securing adequate government funding for it has been difficult. One thorny issue involves the availability of regularly scheduled mammograms for women under fifty. In December 1993 the government-sponsored National Cancer Institute (NCI) announced that it no longer recommends this screening precaution for women in their forties. The NCI's policy change was in accordance with the opinions of a number of health care economists and planners, as well as with President Clinton's new health care proposal.

The National Cancer Institute based its position on thirty years of studies indicating that while regularly scheduled mammograms are a proven lifesaving cancer detection tool for women over fifty, the same did not hold true for younger females. Critics of these studies argue, however,

*Iowa Democratic Senator Tom Harkin has been
extremely helpful in securing increased funding
for breast cancer research.*

that too few women in their forties were involved and that there was inadequate follow-up of study participants. So far the American College of Radiology and the American Cancer Society have continued to recommend such screening for women in their forties, adding that the research has not conclusively ruled out the potential benefits of mammography for females in this age bracket.

Nevertheless, some health care planners insist that the question of cost cannot be negated in such instances. As Dr. David Eddy, professor of health policy and management at Duke University in Durham, North Carolina, and a member of the Clinton health care team, viewed the predicament, "If we yield every time there's a constituency that can make an emotional argument for coverage of something that is not supported by actual evidence, then we will have a chaotic, expensive, and inefficient health care system in this country."[13] Similar sentiments were voiced by Dr. Arleen Leibowitz, a health care economist at the Rand Corporation in Santa Monica, California, who reminded Americans that breast cancer prevention and detection have an inescapable price tag when she said, "We are beginning now to step back and ask, 'How do we want to spend these dollars that are partly public dollars? It's sad to say, but as a society there are some things we cannot do.'"[14]

Yet breast cancer advocates for whom mammograms were essential prior to their turning fifty are ardently opposed to the cost-saving measures recommended by the National Cancer Institute. With the United States "so anguished and angry about breast cancer, it's going to be difficult to remove this tool," warned Amy Langer, executive director of the National Alliance of Breast Cancer Organizations.[15] Advocates also stress that the government's hesitancy to cover the cost of mammograms would unduly punish poor women, who are less likely to be able to pay for such tests on their own.

Dr. Sarah Fox, an associate professor of family medicine at the University of California at Los Angeles, believes both public and private insurers should subsidize regular mammograms for women in their forties, because in surveying women and their physicians she found that cost is the main reason numerous women forgo mammogram screening. Fox fears that denying health care coverage for such procedures pits affluent women against those of lesser means. "We will be enforcing a two-tier medical system," Dr. Fox noted. "That's the direction we wanted to get away from in the Clinton health system." Regarding the uncertain value of this screening for younger women, Fox asks, "Shouldn't we rather be safe than sorry?"[16]

Breast cancer advocates refuse to back down on their demands. As a spokesperson for the movement described their stance:

> *What you have now is a very powerful group of women who are extremely angry and frustrated that very little is known about breast cancer. Women will not stand for the government or*

others to try to take away the only tool we have that is a proven intervention. Maybe it's not good enough, but it's the best we have.[17]

To achieve their funding and strategy goals, breast cancer activists have employed a variety of techniques, including lobbying public officials, launching educational campaigns, and capturing the news media's attention. They've held walkathons, marches, rallies, and demonstrations; gathered signatures for petitions; and waited hours for the opportunity to address legislators. At times they've resorted to dramatic gestures to drive their point home. Acknowledging that being patient and polite hasn't always gotten them what they wanted, one activist claimed that at extremely frustrating moments she's felt like pelting indifferent bureaucrats with breast prostheses.

Especially stirring statements regarding breast cancer have been made by Matuschk, the artist and breast cancer activist who uses "before and after" mastectomy sculptures and photographs of herself to convey the often shocking reality of the disease. She documents the illness's ravages through her art to prevent the public from denying breast cancer's cost to women.

Her message became graphically clear in the summer of 1993, when one of Matuschk's self-photos blatantly exposing her mastectomy scar appeared on the cover of the Sunday *New York Times Magazine*. As might be expected, the startling image evoked a flood of letters and phone calls to the paper. Some felt the work invaded the privacy of other women who'd had mastectomies. But most readers applauded the talented artist for showing that women can survive breast cancer while refusing to allow society to look the other way, as it has in the past.

Despite what some might already regard as success, breast cancer activists have increased their demands and refused to lessen the pressure on either the medical establishment or elected officials. To their credit, government funding for breast cancer research now exceeds amounts allotted for any other malignancy including lung cancer which kills more women annually. The activists argue, however, that while smoking has been identified and highly publicized as a major cause of lung cancer, the causal factors in breast cancer are still uncertain. Defending their position, breast cancer activist Amy Langer noted, "Because so little is known about what's normal, about why cancer cells react the way they do and how we can control them, research is vital."[18] To underscore our limited knowledge about breast cancer, she posed the question, "Why does cancer stop responding to some chemotherapy and why does chemotherapy knock out some cells but not all of them?"[19]

Skeptics think that even large doses of funding may not guarantee the answers they seek. Sociologist Ann Flood at Dartmouth Medical School observed, "People say that money will save lives, but that's not necessarily true. It's not like we

Men and women band together against a devastating disease. Notice the sign stressing that all women are at risk.

are close to brand-new information that would benefit from such funds."[20]

But breast cancer organizers feel differently. They insist that money, public attention, and government support will eventually help conquer this dreaded disease. They believe that adequate funding for breast cancer research will both answer their most pressing questions and shed light on more innovative approaches to combating the illness. "Basically, all cancer is genetic," argued one breast cancer specialist who agrees with the activists. "It's not all hereditary, but it's all genetic. What that means is, it's all a gene that screws up." Explaining that carcinogens interfere with normal genes, she added, "What are these carcinogens in breast cancer? We don't have a clue. Could they be hormones? Sure. Could they be a virus? Sure. It could be pesticides, food additives, or a million other things."[21]

In any case, these women will no longer tolerate being overlooked. Sherry Kohlenberg, who bravely spoke at the Washington, D.C., rally, met with President and Mrs. Clinton in June 1993 to personally argue the cause. By then it was obviously too late for her, but she spoke for the millions of other women who'll be stricken by the disease. Sherry Kohlenberg died the following month, having fought to the end to defeat the foe that invaded her body. As she promised that day at the rally, she did not go silently into that dark night. Now countless women are doing the same.

GLOSSARY

Aspiration — a type of biopsy (see below) in which a needle or syringe is used to either remove fluid from a cyst or cells from a mass.

Benign — not cancerous.

Biopsy — removal of a sample of tissue or cells to be examined under a microscope for diagnostic purposes.

Breast Self-Examination (BSE) — an examination of one's own breasts to note any changes in how they look or feel.

Calcification — small deposits of calcium in tissue, sometimes detectable on mammograms, which may be an early sign of cancer.

Computed Tomography (CT scanning) — an imaging technique using a computer to organize information from multiple X-ray views to construct a cross-sectional image of the breast.

Estrogen — a female hormone involved in breast development. Scientists suspect that estrogen may promote the growth of some types of breast cancer.

Hormones — chemicals manufactured by various glands in the body that specifically affect targeted organs and tissues.

Invasive Cancer — cancer that has spread into and destroyed nearby tissues.

Laser Scanning — breast cancer detection technique being developed in which laser beams and camera imaging are used to scan breast tissue.

Mammogram — an X ray of the breast.

Menopause — the time at which a woman's monthly menstrual periods stop. Menopause is sometimes referred to as the "change of life."

Menstruation — the discharge of blood and tissue from a woman's uterus that occurs monthly during her reproductive years.

Metastasis — the spread of cancer from one part of the body to another.

Palpation — manually feeling for lumps or other irregularities in the breast.

Rad (radiation absorbed dose) — a unit of measurement for radiation.

Radiologist — a doctor especially trained in the use of X rays to image body tissues and treat disease.

Risk Factors (for breast cancer) — conditions or agents that increase a person's likelihood of developing the disease.

Tamoxifen — a drug used in hormone therapy to treat breast cancer.

Tumor — an abnormal tissue growth that may be either malignant or benign.

Tumor markers (for breast cancer) — substances in the blood or other body fluids that may serve as indicators for the presence of the disease.

ORGANIZATIONS CONCERNED WITH CANCER

American Association for Cancer Education
Box 700, UAB Station
Birmingham, AL 35294

American Cancer Society (ACS)
1599 Clifton Road, NE
Atlanta, GA 30329

American Joint Committee on Cancer
55 East Erie Street
Chicago, IL 60611

American Society of Clinical Oncology
435 North Michigan Avenue, Suite 1717
Chicago, IL 60611-4067

American Society of Preventive Oncology
1300 University Avenue, 7C
Madison, WI 53706

Association of American Cancer Institutes
Elm & Carlton Streets
Buffalo, NY 14263

Association of Community Cancer Centers
11600 Nebel Street, Suite 201
Rockville, MD 20852

Breast Cancer Advisory Center
P.O. Box 224
Kensington, MD 20895

Cancer Care
1180 Avenue of the Americas
New York, NY 10036

Cancer Federation, Inc.
21250 Box Springs Road, No. 209
Moreno Valley, CA 92387

Cancer Guidance Institute
1323 Forbes Avenue, Suite 200
Pittsburgh, PA 15219

Cancer Information Service
Boy Scout Building, Room 340
900 Rockville Pike
Bethesda, MD 20892

Chemotherapy Foundation
183 Madison Avenue, Room 403
New York, NY 10016

Damon Runyon - Walter Winchell Cancer
Research Fund
131 East 35th Street
New York, NY 10016

International Society for Preventive Oncology
217 East 85th Street, Suite 303
New York, NY 10028

Make Today Count
101 1/2 South Union Street
Alexandria, VA 22314

National Alliance of Breast Cancer Organizations
1180 Avenue of the Americas, 2nd Floor
New York, NY 10036

National Coalition for Cancer Survivorship
323 8th Street, SW
Albuquerque, NM 87102

National Foundation for Cancer Research
7315 Wisconsin Avenue, Suite 500W
Bethesda, MD 20814

R.A. Bloch Cancer Foundation
H & R Block Building
4410 Main
Kansas City, MO 64110

Reach to Recovery (Cancer)
c/o American Cancer Society

1599 Clifton Road, NE
Atlanta, GA 30329

Society for the Study of Breast Disease
Sammons Tower
3409 Worth
Dallas, TX 75246

Susan G. Komen Breast Cancer Foundation
5005 LBJ, Suite 730
Dallas, TX 75246

United Cancer Council
8009 Fishback Road
Indianapolis, IN 46298-1047

Y-Me National Organization for Breast Cancer
Information and Support
18220 Harwood Avenue
Homewood, IL 60430

SOURCE NOTES

CHAPTER 1

1. Claudia Glenn Dowling, "Fighting Back," *Life*, May 1994, p. 88.
2. E.F. Feuer, "The Lifetime Risk of Developing Breast Cancer," *Journal of the National Cancer Institute*, June 2, 1993, p. 892.
3. Janice Hopkins Tanne, "Everything You Need to Know about Breast Cancer, But Were Afraid To Ask," *New York*, October 11, 1993, p. 55.
4. "Confronting Breast Cancer," *Technology Review*, May/June 1993, p. 53.
5. Traci Watson, "Breast Cancer's Deadly Masquerade," *U.S. News & World Report*, February 7, 1994, p. 60.
6. Tanne.
7. David Schrieberg, "Mother's Breasts," *Mother Jones*, November/December 1992, p. 64.
8. "Confronting Breast Cancer."

9. David Schrieberg.

10. *Ibid.*

11. *Ibid.*

12. *Ibid.*, p. 70.

13. *Ibid.*

14. *Ibid.*, p. 72.

15. *Ibid.*

CHAPTER 2

1. Claudia Glen Dowling, "Fighting Back," *Life*, May 1994, 88.

2. Janice Hopkins Tanne, "Everything You Need to Know about Breast Cancer, But Were Afraid to Ask," *New York*, October 11, 1993, p. 62.

3. *Ibid.*

4. "Confronting Breast Cancer," *Technology Review*, May/June 1993, p. 48.

5. *Ibid.*, p. 49.

6. "Breast Cancer Treatment: Wide Variations by Region of the Country," *Health Facts*, May 1992, p. 2.

7. "Confronting Breast Cancer."

8. Dowling, p. 84.

9. Mango Kaufman, "Cancer Facts vs. Feelings," *Newsweek*, April 24, 1989, p. 10.

10. *Ibid.*

11. *Ibid.*

CHAPTER 3

1. Claudia Glenn Dowling, "Fighting Back," *Life*, May 1994, p. 85.

2. *Oprah* transcript, "What Women Deny to Their Death," August 1, 1994.

CHAPTER 4

1. Claudia Glenn Dowling, "Fighting Back," *Life*, May 1994, p. 85.
2. Susan Ferraro, "The Anguished Politics of Breast Cancer," *The New York Times* Magazine, August 1, 1993, p. 27.
3. *Ibid.*
4. *Ibid.*
5. Steven Finlay, "The Big Scare: Nancy Reagan's Time Comes," *U.S. News and World Report*, October 26, 1987, p. 16.
6. Susan Ferraro.
7. *Ibid.*
8. *Ibid.*
9. "New Report on Breast Cancer," *Health Facts*, February 1992, p. 1.
10. *Ibid.*
11. Susan Ferraro.
12. *Ibid.*, p. 29.
13. Gina Kolata, "Mammogram Debate Moving from Test's Merits to It's Cost," *The New York Times*, December 27, 1993, A1.
14. *Ibid.*
15. *Ibid.*
16. *Ibid.*, p. A14.
17. *Ibid.*
18. Susan Ferraro, p. 31.
19. *Ibid.*
20. Christine Gorman, "Breast Cancer Politics," *Time*, November 1, 1993, p. 74.
21. Susan Ferraro, p. 32.

FURTHER READING

Anderson, Guy. *Essential Things to Do When the Doctor Says It's Cancer.* New York: NAL/Plume, 1993.

Cukier, Daniel and Mc Cullough, Virginia. *Coping with Radiation Therapy: A Ray of Hope.* Los Angeles, California: Lowell House, 1993.

Dranov, Paula. *Estrogen: Is It Right for You? A Thorough Factual Guide to Help You Decide.* New York: Simon & Schuster, 1993.

Feldman, Gayle. *You Don't Have to Be Your Mother.* New York: Norton, 1994.

Ginzberg, Eli. *The Road to Reform: The Future of Health Care in America.* New York: Free Press, 1994.

Kemeny, M. Margret and Dranov, Paula. *Breast Cancer & Ovarian Cancer.* Reading, Massachusetts: Addison-Wesley, 1992.

McGinn, Kerry A. and Haylock, Pamela I. *Women's Cancers: How to Prevent Them, How to Treat Them, How to Beat Them.* Alameda, California: Hunter House, 1993.

Rosenberg, Steven and Barry, John. *The Transformed Cell: Unlocking the Mysteries of Cancer.* New York: Putnam, 1992.

Steen, Grant. *A Conspiracy of Cells: The Basic Science of Cancer.* New York: Plenum, 1993.

INDEX

Cervical cancer, 24
Chemical pollutants, 28
"Chemoprevention," 79
Chemotherapy, 60–62
Clinton, Hillary, 96
Clinton, President Bill, 89, 91, 96
Colony stimulating factors, 64
Computerized tomography (CT), 37

Davis, Dr. Devra Lee, 87
Dehumanizing treatment, 68
Denial, 40–49, 70
Diagnosis, 13–49, 50–51 70–71
Diet, 21–23, 65
    fat in, *21*, 76–78
Drug treatment. *See* Chemotherapy
Ductal carcinoma, 14

Eddy, Dr. David, 91
Eikenberry, Jill, 82
Ellerbee, Linda, 13
Emotional problems, 65, 67–69
Environmental contaminants, 26–28, 65, 87
"Environmental estrogens," 27–28
Estrogen, 23, 27–29, 63
    See also Tamoxifen
Ethnic origin, 25
Exercise, 77, 80, 87

Eye damage, 63

Falck, Frank, Jr., 26–27
Family history, 18–19
First You Cry, 84
Flood, Ann, 94
Ford, Betty, 84
4-PHR, 79
Fox, Dr. Sarah, 92
Fred Hutchinson Cancer Research Center, 19
Frisch, Rose, 77

Gene research, 65
Genetic changes, 38–39
Genetics, 49, 96

Hair loss, 60, 62
Halsted radical mastectomy, 52–54
Harkin, Tom, 88, *90*
Health insurance, 69, 92
Hormones, 23–24, 27–28
Hormone therapy, 62–63, 87

Immunotherapy, 64–65
Income level, 25
Industrial chemicals, 27–28
Infections, 60, 62
Infertility, 62

Japanese Americans, 21, *22*
Jewish women, 25
Journal of the National Cancer Institute, 41–42

110

Kline, Dr. David W., 54
Kohlenberg, Sherry, 83, 96

Langer, Amy, 92, 94
Laser beam scanning, 38
Leibowitz, Dr. Arleen, 91
Life expectancy, 18
Lifestyle, 25
Liver cancer, 15
Lobular carcinoma, 14, 16
Long Island study, 28
Love, Dr. Susan, 29, 42,
  56–57, 85
Lumpectomy, 52–54, 58
  vs. mastectomy, 53–
  56
Lumps, 30, 32–33, 37, 39–
  40
Lung cancer, 14
Lymphatic system, 14
Lymphedema, 53

Magnetic response imag-
  ing (MRI), 37
Malignant tumors, 14
Mammograms, 33, 35, 36,
  44, 47, 76, 89, 91
  cost of, 92–93
  delaying of, 41
  incorrect results,
  48
Mammography Quality
  Standards Act, 35
Mastectomy, 50, 52–54,
  70–73, 79–80
Matuschk, 93
McCormick, Dr. Beryl, 56

Medical establishment, 73–
  74, 86–87
Medical history, 18
Menopause, 19, 23–24, 28,
  30, 62
Menstruation, 19, 23–24,
  30
Mental health, 69
Metastasis, 43, 45
Microcalcification, 33
Misdiagnosis, 48, 73–74

National Alliance of Breast
  Cancer Organizations,
  92
National Breast Cancer
  Coalition, 83, 85, 88,
  89
National Cancer Institute,
  (NCI), 13, 18, 54, 65,
  66, 76, 89, 91– 93
Needle aspiration, 93
Needle biopsy, 39–40
Newman, Phyllis, 70
New York City Health
  Department, 48
New York State Depart-
  ment of Health, 28
Nurses Health Study, 21

Offit, Dr. Kenneth, 18
Oncology, 45, 67
Oral contraceptives, 24
Ovary removal, 63
Ovulation, 23–24

Palpation, 32–33